DEXTER'S INK

BY HOWIE DEWIN

STORY BY AMY KEATING ROGERS AND CHRIS SAVINO

BASED ON "DEXTER'S LABORATORY," AS CREATED BY GENNDY TARTAKOVSKY

SCHOLASTIC INC.

New York   Toronto   London   Auckland   Sydney
Mexico City   New Delhi   Hong Kong   Buenos Aires

special thanks to veronica Ambrose, Allison kaplinsky, sophia psomiadis, maria stasavage and Joe williams for making this book possible.

ISBN 0-439-38579-2

Cover and interior illustrations by John Kurtz
Designed by Maria Stasavage

12 11 10 9 8 7 6 5 4 3 2 1   2 3 4 5 6 7/0

Printed in the U.S.A.
First Scholastic printing, April 2002

"Dexter! I asked you to vacuum the hallway!" Dexter's mother called to him. She stood at the bottom of the stairs with her arms crossed, tapping her foot.

"Dexter! You're also supposed to mow the lawn today!" called his dad.

"And his room is a mess, too!" added Dexter's sister Dee Dee as she danced around the house.

Upstairs, Dexter, boy genius, was hard at work. He was hidden away in his secret laboratory located through an entrance behind his bedroom bookcase. He ignored his mother's call and his father's holler. He paid no attention to his pesky sister, Dee Dee. Instead, Dexter concentrated on the robot he was adjusting.

Dexter's lab was quite an amazing place. It had a huge computer and was filled with high-tech robots. Powerful chemicals bubbled and brilliant machines whirred. The lab had taken Dexter a long time to build. Now it was done. Now he could devote his time to the creation of SCIENCE!

Dexter's family continued to call for him. And he continued to ignore them.

He was very busy with his project. Nothing else concerned him.

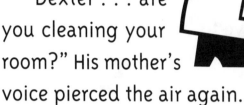

"Dexter . . . are you cleaning your room?" His mother's voice pierced the air again.

"How about washing the car?" yelled Dad.

"And the sink sure is dirty," nagged Dee Dee.

And the one thing that really didn't concern him was stupid housework!

"Yes, Dexter! The bathroom sink needs to be scrubbed!" confirmed Mom.

Screech! Dexter's wrench slipped and scraped across his precious robot.

"How dare they interrupt my brilliant

Science with their mundane tasks!" Dexter exclaimed. "I was nearly finished with my final adjustments to the D-240. Now, thanks to my family's distracting calls, I will have to begin again."

Dexter paced the floor of his lab. He was very frustrated.

"I, Dexter, boy genius, am incredibly busy in the pursuit of Science. I cannot be bothered by such stupid and menial tasks as cleaning my room! Cleaning is for other people! Not for a boy genius! I must find a solution! Through Science!"

"Dexter! It's time to do your chores, dear!" his mother called again.

"Aaauugghhh! Chores! Chores! I have no time for chores!" Dexter threw up his arms. He began counting off on his

fingers all the important things he had to do.

"I have to upgrade my high-speed Zip-drive super-disk, recalibrate my super-conductor electron thruster, and observe my double-fast time-warp gene splicer!"

He stopped in his tracks.

"I have no time for cleanser or sponges or dirty cars or grimy sinks. I have no time for vacuumers of the rug and mowers of the lawn. No time for —"

Just then, Dexter heard his mother's footsteps on the stairs.

"Dexter! I'm coming up to get you, young man!"

"Oh no! Mom! She cannot find me in my secret lab!"

Dexter bolted through the bookcase, back to his bedroom. The last thing he needed was his mother discovering his top secret laboratory. It was bad enough that Dee Dee had figured out how to get in. She was always interrupting his work.

Dexter bolted through the bookcase and closed it just as his mother opened his bedroom door. He fell to his knees and grabbed a pile of dirty laundry from the floor.

"DEXTER!" Mom said with a stern look.

"Heh, heh, heh . . . hello, Mother. I am just straightening up my room as you

requested," Dexter replied meekly.

"That's my boy!" Mom said with a smile. "Here, let me take those."

She took the laundry from Dexter and wrapped it into a bundle.

"Now, you keep doing your chores, son. We need this place tip-top!" Mom began humming happily as she turned to

go. But something caught her eye.

"Oh, Dexter!" she said, sounding disappointed.

"What is it, Mother?" Dexter asked innocently. He was pretending to straighten his bed.

"Now, dear, if I've told you once, I've told you a thousand times. . . ."

Mom held up one of his lab coats. At the base of the pocket was a huge ink stain. Dexter had forgotten to cap one of his pens again. It had leaked all over his coat.

"I'm sorry, Mother," Dexter

said, his head hanging low.

"I should make you write me a letter of apology," Mom said cheerily. "But I doubt you have a pen with any ink left!" She handed him a piece of paper. "Now, here's your list of chores. Get to work!" She shut the door.

"List of chores!" he muttered. "Apology letter! Huh! I should write a resignation letter. I should resign from this family due to unfair child labor laws! Why should a boy of my superior intelligence spend any time on housework? Housework should be done by the less intelligent of this household — Mom, Dad, and especially Dee Dee! I should write down my own list of chores for everyone else in the house to do!"

Dexter's eyes grew wide. What a
brilliant idea! He ran back to his lab.
Finally! He had come up with the
solution!

Chapter 2

"Yes!" declared Dexter triumphantly. "I will no longer be bothered by these most ridiculous of tasks. Once I have created my new invention, I will only have to write down a person's name next to the task I wish for *them* to do and *snap!* They will perform the task and I will be free to think important, universe-altering thoughts!"

Dexter gathered his tools and chemicals. He laid out all his equipment on his worktable. Then he climbed onto his stool and went to work.

He hunched over his latest and greatest invention for hours. He carefully measured a bubbling cup of toxic vapor. He poured the vapor into a little dish. Then he pulled a smoking tablet from a glass jar with a pair of tweezers. He laid the tablet in the little dish. The vapor transformed into a dark liquid. He carefully walked the dish over to his deep-freeze unit and placed it on a shelf by itself.

"Yes! The ink is complete! Everything is going just as I planned. All that remains is some simple welding to create a container for the liquid. Once that is done, I will never do another chore as long as I live. I, Dexter, boy genius, am guaranteed success!" Dexter muttered gleefully to himself.

He picked up a sheet of shiny, clean metal. He skillfully melted down the metal and shaped it into a writing pen.

"I must allow the ink just the right amount of time in the deep-freeze chamber," Dexter said, checking his watch. "The subzero arctic conditions of my hypothermia machine will force a chemical transformation. The simple high-quality writing ink I have created will become —"

Dexter paused to laugh "—hypnosis ink!"

"De-e-ex-ter-r-r!"

"Oh! The nightmare that is my life!" Dexter ran toward the laboratory door. "Dee Dee! Please go away! For I, Dexter, am not here!"

"Yes you are, Dexter! That's how you were able to tell me you weren't here!" Dee Dee danced into the lab in leaps and bounds. There was no time to stop her.

"Dee Dee, you are not welcome in my laboratory! Please leave now. I am at a very inconvenient point to be bothered by a ballet-dancing blond-haired pest who happens to be my sister!"

"What are you doing, Dexter? You're supposed to be cleaning your room and washing the car and mowing the lawn

and scrubbing the sink and vacuuming the hall!"

Dee Dee danced around the lab as she sang out Dexter's long list of chores. "Ooooh! What's this?" she cried.

She picked up the metal that Dexter had made into the shape of a pen.

"That is nothing! You should not be interested in touching that. You should leave me and my laboratory this minute!"

Dee Dee shook the empty pen in frustration.

"You're right, Dexter! This stupid pen doesn't even work!"

She tossed it at Dexter and went leaping toward the door.

"If you don't come do all your chores now, Dexter, then I'll have to do them. And if I do all your chores, I'll probably get tired. And when I get tired, I get confused and babble on and on about anything that comes into my head. And

then I just might tell Mom and Dad all about — you know what!"

"No!" cried Dexter. "Dee Dee! You cannot tell Mom and Dad about my laboratory!"

Dee Dee giggled. She pranced out the door. The bookcase came down and, at last, she was gone.

Dexter looked desperately at the clock. "I have no more time to spare! I must complete my invention now or I will be ruined. Either I will become a slave to lowly housework or my precious laboratory will be revealed! Nnnnoooo!"

He ran to the deep-freeze machine and grabbed the small dish. The liquid inside sparkled like it was mixed with diamonds.

"Perfect! The ink has reached its critical mass. Now all I must do is pour my hypnotizing ink into my pen and —"

Dexter used a funnel to get every drop of his powerful solution inside the pen. He twisted the top onto the pen and set it on the table. The pen began to glow, as if by magic. But it wasn't magic. It was Science! Dexter raised his arms in victory.

"Success! I have done it! I have freed myself from bondage!"

 He grabbed the pen. Carefully but quickly he wrote down the names of all his family members. Then, by each

name, he wrote down one of his boring, pathetic assignments:

Dad	MOW THE LAWN
Mom	VACUUM THE HALL
Dee Dee	SCRUB THE SINK, WASH THE CAR, CLEAN MY ROOM!

Dexter left his lab filled with excitement. He couldn't wait to see his newest invention in action!

Chapter 3

Dexter returned to his bedroom through the bookcase, still clutching his new list of chores. He looked around as he quietly lowered the bookcase to the floor. There were no signs that his invention was working. His room looked exactly the same as it had before — messy.

He reread his list:

"Why is Dee Dee not doing as I command? My inventions do not fail. I am Dexter, boy genius. My hypnosis ink must work. My calculations were exact. My timing was precise! I do not understand."

He began to open the door to the hall-way, but then he stopped himself.

"What if the impossible has happened? What if the pen really doesn't work? Impossible, I know, but . . . what if? I will play it safe," Dexter

said to himself. "I mustn't risk Mom or Dad seeing me until I have proof that my invention works. I will take this bag of trash out into the hall as if I am emptying the garbage."

Dexter grabbed the garbage out of his trash can and emerged from his room. Nobody was around. The hallway still needed to be vacuumed.

Dexter tiptoed to the top of the stairs. His heart was heavy. He did not like the thought of failure. After all, it rarely happened. But it appeared that no one was doing his chores. His shoulders drooped as he headed down the stairs toward the garbage cans in the garage.

"I suppose I should collect the proper cleaning supplies so that while I am in the

garage I can perform my chore of washing the car. Aaauuughh!" Dexter was becoming very depressed. "My time will never be my own!"

He lifted his heavy feet down the stairs. When he reached the bottom step, he was suddenly spun in circles.

It was Dee Dee. "Pardon me, Dexter!" she exclaimed. She was dancing even faster than usual. "But I have so much to do and so little time! I have to clean your

room and, by the way, I'm sorry it's taking me so long, but I had to scrub the sink and wash the car and —"

Just then, something bumped against Dexter. It was his mother, pulling the vacuum along behind her. "Oh! I'm sorry, son. The vacuum cleaner can be such a bother!" she said. "But what can I do? I MUST vacuum the hall!"

Dexter felt the lump in his stomach disappear in an instant. It had worked! His pen was a success!

"How ridiculous that I doubted my-self!" he said, dropping the garbage bag. "Of course it works! I am a boy genius! I am a FREE boy genius!"

He took out the pen and wrote down a new chore for his sister:

"Oh!" Dee Dee exclaimed. "First things first, Dexter. I'll get to your room in a minute. But now, I must take out this trash!"

Dee Dee swooped past Dexter and whisked the trash away.

"Oh, the joy of Science! Oh, the elation!" Dexter cried with glee. His first instinct was to rush back to his lab, but he decided to check on his dad. As a scientist, he had an obligation to confirm all the results of his experiment.

He peered out the garage window. Dad was behind the lawn mower, whipping around the yard like a maniac.

Dexter turned back to look at his mother. It was as if she were in a trance. She was vacuuming the hall as cheerful as could be. That gave Dexter another idea. He pulled out his list and wrote:

Mom MAKE ALL OF DEXTER'S FAVORITE FOODS

He had barely finished writing before his mother dropped the vacuum cleaner. She headed straight for the kitchen.

"Time to clean Dexter's room! Time to clean Dexter's room!" Dee Dee was heading back into the house, singing happily. A silly grin was on her face.

The whole family was totally hypnotized! "Excellent!" Dexter said to himself. "And now I must return to my laboratory and continue the very important work that is my life."

For once, he wasn't worried about Dee Dee following him into his lab. She had been told what to do and was obeying. She was too busy cleaning his room to pester him.

Dexter could not stop grinning as he settled back onto his stool. He pulled out a glass beaker and got to work. It was so nice to be left alone!

But unfortunately, Dexter was not as alone as he thought. Only a few blocks away, his greatest rival sat in his own laboratory. Mandark stared at a large monitor on the wall. He was very pleased with himself. He had snuck into Dexter's lab one night while his rival slept. Then he had installed a hidden camera. One by one, he had disabled the lab's security measures. Now he could spy on Dexter whenever he wanted — and steal all of the boy genius's inventions! And right now, he was determined to steal that latest and greatest invention — the hypnosis pen.

Chapter 4

Dexter worked away in his lab. He was very happy. No one would bother him in his laboratory. And when he finished with his hard work for the day, he would return to a spotlessly clean room. Life was perfect.

But Mandark had other ideas. As he gazed at Dexter and his newest invention,

Mandark began to imagine how wonder-ful his life would be if he had the hypnosis pen.

"I could finally achieve my greatest dream," Mandark said. "I could hypnotize Dexter and instruct him to destroy his own lab! Ha-ha-ha! Ha-ha-ha-ha-ha!" Mandark laughed evilly. He began to pace back and forth as he plotted against his rival.

Back in his lab, Dexter was winding down after a hard day of Science.

"Never before has my genius been quite so obvious. I have created the most perfect invention in history! Now I have all the time in the world for SCIENCE!" Dexter picked up the pen and held it up so that it sparkled in the light. Then, he yawned.

"I am completely exhausted from my mental exertions. For the first time in months — no, years — I have had no interruptions from my sister, Dee Dee! What a glorious feeling! But now it is time for bed, for tomorrow is yet another day for Science!"

Dexter put down the pen and headed to bed. Back in his room, he looked around and smiled with satisfaction. It was just as he'd hoped. The room was sparkling clean.

"Well, at last, my dancing pest of a sister has done something worthwhile.

She is quite good at housecleaning!"

Dexter yawned again and stretched out on his bed. In no time, he was fast asleep, a smile of contentment on his face.

In fact, Dexter slept so soundly that he didn't hear the floorboard creak as Mandark slipped by him. Dexter's rival had skillfully eluded all of his security systems. Mandark lifted the bookcase just

high enough to slip into Dexter's secret lab. He was in!

"Ha-ha-ha!" Mandark cackled with satisfaction. He had always told Dexter that this lab was small and unimpressive compared to his own. But it was also true that Mandark was very jealous of Dexter's inventions. Mandark hated competition. He had to stop Dexter the only way he could — by destroying his lab.

Mandark surveyed the laboratory thoughtfully. His eyes fell upon the pen. "Dexter! You are a fool! For you foolishly left your latest invention — the hypnosis pen — out in the open for me, Mandark, to find. And now that I have found it, you, Dorkster, will be under my control! Ha-ha-ha! Ha-ha-ha-ha-ha!" Mandark

declared. His eyes glistened with an evil gleam.

In an instant, Mandark had grabbed the pen. Then he snatched a piece of paper and began to write.

Chapter 5

As soon as the sun rose the next morning, Dexter's eyes popped open. But there was something different about them. They had the same dazed, hypnotized look that Dee Dee's had had yesterday. Dexter was definitely not himself.

"I have no time to spare," Dexter said calmly. "I must disassemble the Magnum D-240, disengage my spectron monitor,

37

take down the power grid, and delete my complete collection of backup files."

Dexter grabbed a clean lab coat from his closet.

"In short," he continued, "I must destroy my lab. I must do it and I must do it right away."

Dexter moved quickly and smoothly. He was almost like a robot. He slipped by the bookcase and headed to the heart of his laboratory.

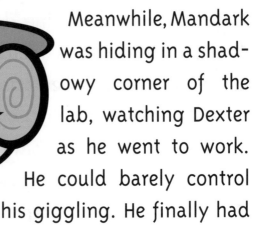

Meanwhile, Mandark was hiding in a shadowy corner of the lab, watching Dexter as he went to work. He could barely control his giggling. He finally had

Dexter just where he wanted him.

"It's clear who is the greatest genius now!" Mandark whispered to himself. "Any clever boy could invent a hypnosis pen. But it takes a true boy genius to steal it and use it for his ultimate goal — to rule! And what better ruler than I, Mandark, evil boy genius! That Dexter did not appreciate the power he had in his very hands! But now that I have the hypnosis pen, nobody will be safe from the power of ultimate persuasion I possess!"

"Be sure to completely disassemble the laser beam blaster. Leave no bolt screwed in," Dexter muttered to himself as he worked at destroying the thing he cared

most about in the world.

Dexter flung open panels on his computer. He began yanking out red wires, blue wires, and yellow wires. He flipped switches and ground apart microchips with his hammer. His computer monitor flashed a warning as it deleted thousands of files.

Mandark couldn't stop himself. "Ha-ha-ha!" he laughed like a maniac.

But Dexter didn't hear him. He was too busy obeying the command of the hypnosis pen. Mandark could do anything he wanted. Dexter would not stop.

"So simple," cackled Mandark. "So brilliant!"

"De-e-ex-ter-r-r!"

Even the ever-annoying sound of his sister's voice couldn't stop Dexter. But it had a very different effect on Mandark.

He froze where he stood. His jaw dropped open and his eyes grew wide. Now he was hypnotized — not by the pen, but by love. "*Deeee Deeee*," he cooed.

Dee Dee burst into the room. She leaped around, flinging her arms into the air. She danced in a circle before stopping to speak to her brother again.

"De-e-ex-ter-r-r!" she called coyly.

"My love," Mandark sputtered. He felt himself becoming confused and dizzy. This happened every time he saw Dee Dee. He could do nothing but stare. He stepped out from the shadows and fell to his knees.

"Sweet Dee Dee," he cried. As he spoke, the hypnosis pen fell from his hand and clattered across the floor.

Chapter 6

Dee Dee spun around and blinked her big blue eyes. "Oooooooh," she squealed. She had caught sight of the beautiful glowing pen. It didn't look anything like the boring empty pen she'd seen yesterday. "Lovely!"

Mandark nearly fell over. He thought Dee Dee was talking to him. "What?" he asked in disbelief.

"It's the most beautiful thing I've ever seen!"

Mandark saw Dee Dee dancing straight toward him. He opened his arms to embrace her. But Dee Dee didn't stop. She pirouetted right past him and scooped up the pen.

"It's so sparkly. It looks like it's filled with beautiful crystals!" she cried. "I L-O-O-O-O-V-E writing in curly cursive with brand-new beautiful pens! Thank you, Mandark."

Dee Dee sat down at Dexter's table and started doodling. With his genius IQ, Mandark was clever enough to realize what was about to happen. But he couldn't stop it. He wasn't fast enough. He struggled to his feet as Dee Dee doodled his name. She wrote:

Mandark

"Oooh!" Dee Dee squealed again. "What a great pen! It's so smooth and the ink is so pretty!" Then she wrote one of her favorite words:

Pony

Mandark's eyes glazed over. In an instant, he had fallen under the power of the pen. He walked mechanically toward the secret entrance to the lab.

Meanwhile, now that Mandark was no

longer in possession of the pen, Dexter began to come to his senses. He quickly realized that Dee Dee had the pen.

"Dee Dee, no! My invention —" Dexter dove toward his sister, but it was too late. She had just finished writing two more words:

Dexter   Flowers

Dexter stopped in his tracks. He stared blankly. Then he calmly turned away from Dee Dee and walked out the door.

As Dexter was leaving the laboratory, Mandark was returning. But he was not alone. He was leading a beautiful white pony with a perfectly braided mane.

"Pony!" Dee Dee exclaimed.

She jumped up and down with glee, still holding the pen tightly. Behind her, lying on the table, was the paper, which was now covered with many more words. Around *Mandark* Dee Dee had written:

Dollies   Puppies   Ribbons

And around Dexter's name it said:

Rainbows   Candy   Ballerinas

Quick as can be, Mandark dropped the pony's reins and raced out of the lab. On the way he passed Dexter, who was pushing a wheelbarrow overflowing with dozens of different kinds of flowers.

"So many pretty colors!" Dee Dee shouted. "Oooh! I love flowers!"

Mandark returned, dragging a bag twice his size. He turned it upside down and a shower of beautiful baby dolls fell out.

"Dollies!" Dee Dee rejoiced.

Meanwhile, Dexter was hunched over his worktable. He poured three chemicals together in a dish. Suddenly, a glorious rainbow sprang from the dish and streaked through the air. Soon the entire lab was covered in bright reds, yellows, blues, and purples.

"I LLLLLLOOOOVVVVEEEEE dollies and I LLLLOOOVVVVEEE rainbows!" Dee Dee

exclaimed. She was filled with happiness.

Dexter and Mandark couldn't hear her. The barking of five dozen puppies following Mandark into the lab drowned Dee Dee out. The puppies ran straight to the mounds of candy that Dexter was making in his petri dishes. But Dee Dee was even faster, and she got there first.

"*Mmmmmfffoooollllmmmnneeep!*" she said. Her mouth was stuffed with chocolates and marshmallows.

Mandark whizzed by. He was twisted up in yards and yards of brightly colored ribbons and bows. He untangled himself and left the ribbons at Dee Dee's feet.

"Dexter! I just love what you've done with your laboratory! This is sooooo much better than all those boring computers and machines! This is the prettiest place I've ever been!" shrieked Dee Dee.

But Dexter wasn't there to hear Dee

Dee's praise. He was busy instructing ten ballerinas. He was trying to get them to leap through the bookcase and into the lab.

"Ballerinas!" Dee Dee screamed. She leaped straight up in the air. "I'm a ballerina, too! This is like a dream come true!"

Dee Dee spun around the room. She jumped and twirled in circles, shoving handfuls of candy into her mouth all the while. Sixty puppies wrapped in ribbons and bows danced after her. The rainbow sparkled around her and the pony whinnied with pleasure. On and on Dee Dee danced. She had never been more happy.

Dee Dee skipped and whirled and pranced for hours. And she kept the pen

firmly between her fingers the whole time. But finally, she grew tired. She grabbed a red rose from the mound of flowers and collapsed on the mound of supersoft dollies.

"This is perfection!" Dee Dee threw her head back, and the hypnosis pen fell out of her hand.

As if in slow motion, it flew through the air and landed exactly between Dexter and Mandark.

The two boys instantly snapped out of their trances. They looked at the pen. Then they looked at each other for a long moment. And then . . .

"Make way! Boy genius coming through!" Dexter cried as he threw himself at the pen.

"NOOOOOO!" yelled Mandark. "I will prevail!"

Mandark leaped toward the pen, too. Both boys landed hard on the floor next to it.

"*Oooofff!*" Dexter grunted.

"*Uuuuuggg!*" Mandark spat.

There was a split second of silence. Then Dexter raised his hand in the air. The pen was clenched between his fingers.

"I am victorious!" Dexter announced. "I will not relinquish my most valuable of inventions again! You may have fooled me once, Mandark, but I will not be fooled twice. Now you and Dee Dee must leave my laboratory immediately so that I may repair it to normal working order."

"Your victory is temporary," Mandark sneered. "I, Mandark, will prevail!"

Dexter was so mad, he could barely contain himself. "I do not have any more time to spend with the likes of you, Mandark!" he yelled. "The stealing of my invention proves once and for all that I, not you, am the superior scientist."

Dee Dee was looking on with big, baffled blue eyes.

"And you, Dee Dee, have caused nothing but destruction, as usual," Dexter growled at his sister. "You have made my laboratory a disaster zone of girlish nonsense. I will not forgive you for this any time soon. Now go! I banish you!"

Dee Dee and Mandark stood firm. Dexter was about to yell at them again,

when he had a better idea. He grabbed a fresh sheet of paper and scrawled two names on it:

Dee Dee   and   Mandark

He drew a circle around the two names. Then, around the outside of the circle, he wrote:

CLEAN UP AND REBUILD
MY LABORATORY

Without a moment's delay, Dee Dee began picking up ribbons and putting away dollies. Mandark was already reconnecting wires to Dexter's main-frame.

Once again, Dexter sat tall on his work stool. He looked at his pen with pride. It really was one of his greatest inventions. He kicked his feet back for a moment and watched Dee Dee and Mandark clean his lab.

Dee Dee struggled to round up the sixty puppies, and she didn't even stop to rest. She scrubbed the rainbow off the

wall while Mandark reassembled Dexter's robots. It was more than an hour before they were done working. And Dexter's laboratory looked even better than before. Not only was everything neat and orderly, but it was also sparkling clean. Dee Dee had polished every bit of metal. She had even washed all of Dexter's glass beakers!

Now Dexter was ready to get back to work. Science awaited him.

"I cannot wait to have my lab back to myself. These inferior people are sapping me of my mental strength and leaving me unable to create more extraordinary

Scientific wonders! I must remove them from my laboratory."

Dexter pulled the pen out again and wrote:

Dee Dee and Mandark
GO PLAY OUTSIDE AND
LEAVE DEXTER ALONE!

Dee Dee and Mandark instantly stopped what they were doing and ran happily toward the laboratory door.

"Good-bye and good riddance!" Dexter murmured.

Dee Dee and Mandark didn't even stop to say good-bye. They just ran laughing through the bookcase exit and straight out of the house.

"*Eeeegh!*" screeched Monkey, Dexter's lab assistant.

"I couldn't agree with you more," nodded Dexter. "Good riddance again! There is much work to be done!"

Dexter laid down his pen on his desk and went to gather supplies for his next experiment.

Chapter 9

"Oh, it is a glorious thing to have the lab to myself!" exclaimed Dexter, looking with pride at the array of materials before him. "Once again, I can pursue my dream of a life of Science. So much to be invented, so much to be explored!"

Dexter settled into his work. He studied a long equation on his blackboard. Then he moved swiftly to his atom condenser.

He'd just had a brand-new idea and this one might even surpass the hypnosis pen, his greatest idea to date!

"*Eeegh!*" chirped Monkey as Dexter bustled around.

"I cannot work with you today," he told Monkey. "I am hot on the trail of a new invention!"

Dexter was hunched over the condenser when Monkey let out another screech. He was so busy, Dexter didn't see him reach down and grab the beautiful glowing pen. Nor did he see Monkey pull a piece of paper into his cage and write:

DEXTER bring Monkey bananas!

A moment later, Dexter turned around

to face Monkey. There was a funny glaze in the boy genius's eyes. "Must get bananas," Dexter muttered as he headed toward the lab door.

Monkey just grinned and winked.

THE END